The Wolf
Who Wanted to Celebrate his Birthday

Text by Orianne Lallemand
Illustrations by Eleonore Thuillier

AUZOU

One fine afternoon, Alfred knocked on the wolf's door.
"Hi, wolf!" he said. "Come and play soccer with us.
You're the only one who's missing."
"I'd love to," replied the wolf. "And I'll tell you all about
my birthday plans. This year, I'd like to—"
But the wolf stopped short in the middle of his sentence.
Alfred had already scurried off.

By the time the wolf reached the forest,
the game had already begun.
"Hi, Luna! Who's winning?" asked the wolf.
"The red team, unfortunately," Luna replied.
"I think it's time you joined us!"
"I'm coming!" shouted the wolf as he rushed onto the field.

There was a moment when the team was muddled together, but then... a pass by the wolf, a dribble by Alfred, a frightful cry from Miss Yeti and... a goal for the blue team! Hooray!

It was a very close game, but the blue team finally won.
The wolf gathered his friends together to tell them his plans.

"Listen, everyone," he began. "This year, I've decided to celebrate
my birthday with a **mega** party at my home next Saturday.
You're all invited!"
His friends looked uneasily at each other.

"Shucks!" said Valentino. "Lucian's already invited me over to his place next Saturday."
"And I've got a basketball practice that I can't miss," said Alfred. "Sorry!"
"I've got my cooking class on Saturday," added Big Louis.
"And I'm having dinner with Divinia," murmured Luna.

??!!

The wolf could feel his whiskers twitching and 1, 2, 3... he blew his top!

"OK, I get it!" he exclaimed. "Don't worry, we'll celebrate my birthday next year. See you later!"

The angry wolf went to sulk in the forest. He was wandering around, kicking stones and bits of wood, when suddenly... **BOING!**

"Ouch!" cried the wolf, rubbing his paw.
"What on earth was that?" he asked himself as he bent
down to pick up the object.

It was an unusual gold bottle with an elaborately carved stopper.

The wolf was curious. He examined the object closely. What could be inside? He hesitated for a moment and then carefully pulled out the stopper.

SWISH! SWOOSH! WOOSH! A cloud of gold dust escaped from the bottle and a strange bird appeared.

"Hi, wolf!" said the bird. "Today is your lucky day! I'm a genie and I can grant you three wishes. Come on, speak up, I don't have much time!"

The wolf observed the weird creature in amazement.
The timing couldn't have been better.
He was fed up with the forest and his friends.

The Whole
Universe

"I'd like to be somewhere else... far away from here," replied the wolf.
"May your wish come true!" declared the genie.

And with a **SWISH! SWOOSH! WOOSH!** the wolf
disappeared in a cloud of sparkling, gold glitter.

When the wolf woke up, he was on a vast red planet, covered in cracks and stones.

"Welcome to Mars!" shouted the genie.
"It was the furthest place I could find. I hope you're satisfied."
"No, I'm not!" exclaimed the terrified wolf.
"I had, well, um... a prettier landscape in mind."

"Why didn't you say so, kid?" sighed the genie.

And **SWISH! SWOOSH! WOOSH !**

This time, the scenery was much nicer! Bright sunshine, sandy beaches, and a turquoise blue sea...

"There you are!" exclaimed the genie proudly.
"You have this paradise island all to yourself."

The wolf went swimming, nibbled on a snack, took a nap, returned for a swim, nibbled on another snack, and was bored.

"If only my friends were here too," he thought.
But his face soon dropped.
"*Pfff!* They're no doubt having a great time without me."
And he was convinced they were.

The wolf decided to keep himself occupied by exploring the island. It was so exhausting! Not to mention the swarms of mosquitoes getting on his nerves.

"At least there aren't any snakes," he muttered.
"I hate snakes." But just as he spoke, a Papuan python
fell out of a tree and right on the wolf.

Slowly but surely, the enormous reptile started winding itself around the wolf. In one last all-out effort, the wolf managed to turn the bottle upside down and the genie appeared.

"What can I do for you?" he asked.
"A final wish, perhaps?"

"I... ret... urn... ho... home," stammered the trembling wolf.

"So be it!" declared the genie.
"Quite frankly, I expected your third wish to be much more interesting!"

And **SWISH! SWOOSH! WOOSH!**

When the wolf opened his eyes again,
he was back in his forest. Phew!
"There you are!" exclaimed Mr. Owl.
"Where have you been? We've been looking
everywhere for you!"

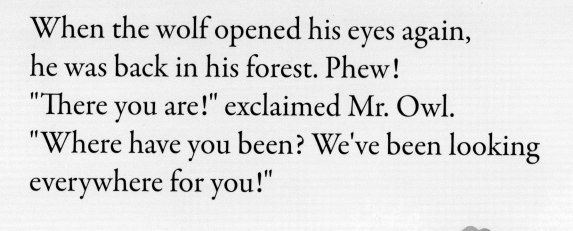

"I... um... I fell asleep under a tree," stammered the wolf.

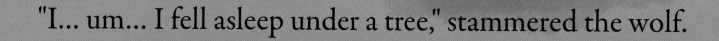

"You mean you went off to sulk!" replied Mr. Owl.
"You and your terrible temper! Now, go home
and don't fall asleep on the way."
The wolf set off in a hurry. He couldn't wait to be back home
and in his cozy, warm bed.

With a sigh of relief, the wolf opened his door. But, then he immediately stopped in his tracks...
There was a huge cardboard box in the middle of his living room.

"**Surprise! HAPPY BIRTHDAY, WOLF!**"
His friends leaped up and showered him with confetti.
The wolf had forgotten that it was his birthday!

"And I thought you didn't care about my birthday,"
he said sheepishly.

"We had already planned on celebrating silly wolf!"
exclaimed Valentino.
"We were only pretending not to care!"

!!!

Luna handed him an envelope. With a startled
and pounding heart, the wolf read the message.

"Dear wolf,

Your birthday present is a week at the beach with all your

closest and dearest friends. Be ready to leave after the party!

From your friends who love you so much."

Grinning from ear to ear, the wolf looked around at his friends.
He wouldn't be in bed early tonight, after all.
But he didn't mind. This was so much the better!

General Director: Gauthier Auzou
Senior Editor: Laura Levy
Layout: Annaïs Tassone and Eloïse Jensen
Production: Lucile Pierret
Translation from French: Susan Allen Maurin
Original title: *Le loup qui fêtait son anniversaire*
© 2015, Auzou Publishing, Paris (France), English Version

Printed and bound in China, August 2015
ISBN : 978-2-7338-3557-9